Samantha Lawrence and the Big Bully

Written and Illustrated by Shannon Lin

少年文學65　PG3062

Samantha Lawrence and The Big Bully

作者／Shannon Lin
插畫／Shannon Lin
責任編輯／孟人玉
圖文排版／許絜瑀
封面設計／Shannon Lin
封面完稿／王嵩賀
出版策劃／秀威少年
製作發行／秀威資訊科技股份有限公司
114 台北市內湖區瑞光路76巷65號1樓
電話：+886-2-2796-3638
傳真：+886-2-2796-1377
服務信箱：service@showwe.com.tw
http://www.showwe.com.tw

郵政劃撥／19563868
戶名：秀威資訊科技股份有限公司
展售門市／國家書店【松江門市】
104 台北市中山區松江路209號1樓
電話：+886-2-2518-0207
傳真：+886-2-2518-0778

網路訂購／秀威網路書店：https://store.showwe.tw
國家網路書店：https://www.govbooks.com.tw
法律顧問／毛國樑　律師

總經銷／聯合發行股份有限公司
231新北市新店區寶橋路235巷6弄6號4F
電話：+886-2-2917-8022
傳真：+886-2-2915-6275

出版日期／2024年6月　BOD一版　**定價**／350元
ISBN／978-626-97570-6-0

讀者回函卡

SAMANTHA LAWRENCE AND THE BIG BULLY

Written and
Illustrated by **SHANNON LIN**

Acknowledgements

I'm grateful for my parents who give me such a caring and full of love support no matter what I do. Especially throughout the whole process of writing the story, they're always there for me! Love you!

Also, thanks to my brother, Nathan, although he doesn't really know what I'm doing, but he always gives me support and love whenever I need it.

Special thanks to my English teacher, Ingrid Wang, for helping me go through the whole story and revise its grammar usage.

Another special thanks to my art teacher, Hui-Ling, who helped me organize my characters and design the illustrations in my story.

Thank you all for helping me to accomplish my first book!!!

Contents

Samantha Lawrence and The Big Bully

Chapter 1
New Day of School

Phew!

It was so hot! Not that the weather was hot, it was just that I was so afraid and nervous to go to school that I was sweating profusely. I was sitting on the porch of my house waiting for my mom to drive the car out of the garage.

It was only seven in the morning, which was pretty early for me. Why do schools start so early, anyways? As I got in the car, I tried to picture what my new school would look like. Yep, new school, you heard it. I originally lived in Chicago, and moved to LA around a month ago during summer vacation, due to my dad's job. We now lived in Silver Lake, where I would be attending my new school called **"Casteral Elementary School."** After waiting for a whole month, I could finally return to school and meet some new friends. All my old friends were still in Chicago. I missed them so much.

Well, voilà, there was my origin story. That was a chapter of my life, and now, I was going to start a new, fresh chapter. I was so ***nexcited*** (nervous + excited)! One thing I was looking forward to trying out was the school cafeteria, which I heard was absolutely delicious! What could I say? I was a diligent foodie who'd done her research.

My new homeroom teacher was Ms. Hayes. She only taught English and social studies. The rest of the subjects were for the other teachers.

When my parents brought my brother, Nate, and me to visit the new school, the principal showed us a picture of Ms. Hayes. She had the kind of "teacher face" you'd see in children's books about school life.

During summer vacation, I didn't really go outside and play dodgeball in my front yard. I was usually cooped inside reading as opposed to playing outside. In the stories that I read, there were some really mean bullies who pretended to be the main character's friends before betraying the main character.

I wanted none of that to happen to me. All I wanted was to be a normal, average girl with many friends at school, and have nothing to do with **meanies**.

I probably already had some of the qualities I needed to transform into the kind of person I wanted in school, but I was still really anxious about starting a new school in an unfamiliar environment. Still, I guessed I was **ALMOST** ready to go to school!

I really liked our school uniforms because they were my favorite colors: blue and white. (I liked pink and purple when I was younger, but I was ten now, so I was too old to like these colors. They're too childish and naïve, you know, kids in my last school weren't really fond of them.)

When I got out of the car, I saw a girl that was wearing all black—a black hoodie, a black skirt, and a pair of black shoes. I was surprised to see that she didn't have a backpack slung over her shoulder. Shouldn't students always be carrying a backpack?

Out of curiosity, I asked her, "Why aren't you wearing your uniform?"

She responded unnecessarily rudely, "Mind your own business, ***DORK***!"

I was taken aback. I was just asking, why was she so rude?

Anyways, I wasn't gonna let this girl I encountered earlier ruin my first day of school. Well, if I was lucky enough, she wouldn't be in the same class as me.

But I found something funny about her. She dressed **exactly** like how one of my old classmates in kindergarten did! That was **strange**! I mean, even the brand of her hoodie (*Barisa* by the way) was the same!

Barisa tops always have a coffee bean logo on their left side, close to the wearer's chest. And that mean girl wore a black Barisa hoodie, similar to that classmate of mine in kindergarten, who also wore that exact same hoodie for every single day. The only difference between those two hoodies was the size.

Nevertheless, this was likely a mere coincidence, so I didn't give it much thought. In spite of this unpleasant run-in with the weird girl, I was determined to make my school life smooth-sailing.

"I, Samantha Park Lawrence, hereby declare that I will get along with everyone and make many friends." I said aloud to myself.

The first period was homeroom.

Ms. Hayes walked in and handed out our books.

"Now kids, here are your textbooks and workbooks for English class. Next, these are your Social Studies textbooks and folders. I will be in charge of teaching you English and Social Studies this year," Ms. Hayes explained.

"Um, how about our materials for science, math, Chinese, music, and all the other stuff?" Asked Grant Holler, whose name I got from his name tag.

"Oh, yes. The other teachers will hand them out to you. I know, this year's different," Ms. Hayes answered.

Many of the girls in school adored Grant, but I had no clue why. I guessed it was because he could play basketball **very well** and was good at math. Well, at least, that was what I overheard from the other girls.

Then, another person raised her hand. This time

it was Jessica Camin. I heard that she had a great personality and got **fabulous grades** in all the subjects. In fact, she was in our school's top five in terms of results!

"Um, Ms. Hayes? Where are our schedules? I'm so desperate to check them right now." Jessica said.

"Oh, right. Thank you for reminding me, Jessica. I'll give them to you right away," Ms. Hayes answered.

After she passed out the schedules, another person raised his hand. It was Joshua Lecut, a boy who was known for his **sharp brains** and very smug facial expressions. Some girls admired him too. As for him, I guessed it was because he was a pro at nearly all the **sports** and that his grades were really high.

"Yes, Joshua?" Ms. Hayes asked.

"Who's that new girl?" He questioned, pointing his index finger at me.

"Oh, right! Sorry, Samantha," she said and addressing the class, continued, "Children, this is our new student, Samantha Lawrence." Ms. Hayes then turned to me and asked, "Samantha, can you stand up and introduce yourself?"

"Okay, I guess. Um, hi everyone! It's nice to meet you guys! I've been looking forward to meeting you and I think I'm very lucky to be here. Thank you," I introduced myself.

"**Welcome**!" A girl named Erica Carter exclaimed.

"Thanks," I said.

The last person who raised her hand was Matilda Welson. A girl whom I wanted to be friends with, after

Samantha
Lawrence
Casteral
Elementary
School
WELCOME!

seeing a picture of her on the "Honor Wall." She was quite pretty, and smart, but apparently could be a little bit bossy. That was what people said anyways. But hey, bossy people were usually just opinionated and they often turned out to be quite protective of their friends. And that was exactly what I needed, ***a protective friend***.

Suddenly, a girl raised her hand. ***It was that rude girl from earlier!*** I was surprised. Then Ms. Hayes called on her.

"Yes, Gemma?" She said, with a hint of annoyance.

Wait a minute, **Gemma**... She was my classmate when I was in kindergarten! I recalled that she was incredibly rude towards me! And I used to be bullied by her! How did I not recognize her?

After realizing that that rude person I encountered earlier was the very same bully of my childhood, I tried to ignore her, but that didn't work out so well. Ignoring her turned out to be more difficult than I imagined. She was so huge and was literally a **black thing** in the middle of the classroom, sucking up all my happiness! I was finally at a new school, yet here I was, classmates with Gemma Hoffman! **Again…** I couldn't believe my rotten luck.

She interjected, "Like, are there any dress codes?"

"Yes, we wear the school uniform on Monday, Tuesday, and Wednesday. And you can wear your own clothes on Thursday and Friday," Ms. Hayes answered, "Gemma, have you forgotten? We've talked about this last semester! **Good gracious!**"

I always wondered. Why did she prefer to wear all black instead of the school uniform? I guessed she was trying to show how counterculture she was, or maybe thought it was cool, or she simply hated our uniform. She was probably the type of person who thinks that the colors of the rainbows reminded her of a pixie fairy barfing on a unicorn cupcake. (Well, if a pixie fairy **REALLY** did barf on a unicorn cupcake, I would try my best to take a picture and honor that moment. Of course, that was just hypothetical.)

When I got home, my parents asked how my first day of school was.

"Well, it was all going okay **UNTIL** I recognized Gemma Hoffman. I can't believe she's my classmate again!" I cried.

I saw my brother shudder. He heard about her from me because I complained about her all the time when I was in kindergarten. Even he was afraid of Gemma!

"***That*** Gemma Hoffman?" My mom asked.

Just as she was trying to recall things about Gemma, I interrupted her.

"Yes, it's her alright! The horrors!"

"Okay, then. Be careful. Don't mess with her." My dad exclaimed, "Try to get along with everyone else, and ignore her."

I guessed my dad was right. I could just ignore her and do the things I want! What difference did it make now that she was here?

When I was eating my dinner, Nate suddenly asked

me a question.

"Do you think she—Gemma—would target you again? Like when you were in kindergarten?"

I started to recall how Gemma bullied me and laughed at me.

"I think she was just jealous. I'm pretty and have good grades and can draw, sing, dance, and so on," I responded smartly.

"Don't act all smug," said my brother, "After all, you have a bad habit."

"Of doing what exactly?" I asked.

"You eat ***veeeery*** slowly!" My brother laughed.

"Well, I'm not as slow as you!" I protested. "Whatever. Just forget it."

"Yeah, yeah. Blah, blah," murmured my brother.

After I finished my dinner, I started to write my homework. We hadn't received much homework on the first day of school, so I was almost finished.

While I was writing, I thought about this:

Being with Gemma every day in the foreseeable future still didn't feel right. I mean, I still didn't know if she would bully me or do something hurtful to me. But I couldn't just avoid her completely during the school year, right?

Chapter 2
Gemma's in Hot Water

A few days passed by, and I became quite the popular girl in school. Well, you could say that most of the students knew my name. Although this wasn't what I was going for, it did feel pretty cool, I admit. Wherever I went, people just kept saying, "**Samantha!** Wow, you're so cool!" Funnily enough, I still didn't know what I was famous for.

Was it my looks? I have to confess, I've never realized how attractive I was until this point… Ha! I was just kidding! But, with all these beauty standards now, I didn't know if I was considered pretty enough for all these judgmental people. Still, I had to be confident about myself, right?

So, back to the main topic, could it be because of my grades? If I was being honest, my grades were indeed utterly amazing. I was complimented by Ms. Hayes three or four times over the past few days! (Wait, was this the part where I should be humble and not praise myself?) Anyways, I did think of another reason.

Fun fact, I could sing, dance, play the piano, and code better than Gemma anyways.

The only problem was, if this was the reason for all my popularity, how did all these people figure out that I had these talents? Did someone spread this news?

I didn't know how everybody knew, but apparently, Gemma was furious at the person who told everybody this, because everyone kept ignoring Gemma. She was **100%** angry, of course. There was even a rumor about Gemma getting kicked out of the principal's office after she complained to him about how the school kept ignoring her. Poor 'lil Gemma Hoffman! I could even feel her anger from her seat, which was kinda far away from mine.

It was Friday, so there was culinary class. During the recess before the class, I was preparing the supplies for culinary class in the homeroom; Jessica, Barrett, Elizabeth, and Amara were reading their own favorite books; Joshua and Easton were chasing after each other; Erica and Aleina, the only ones who were sitting in their own seats, were chatting away while fiddling with their pens; across, Rowan and Isaac were arm wrestling; and beside them, Jacob and Antony were talking about Roblox and Minecraft.

Out of nowhere, Matilda Welson came up to me. I was surprised because she gave me some candy. I asked her what kind of candy it was, and she said that it was brown sugar candy. Brown sugar candy was my favorite, so I ate it.

Suddenly, there was a smelly odor coming from my mouth. The candy tastes spicy and smelled like ginger—***It was ginger candy!***

I was upset. I thought she was trying to be my friend and was using the candy as a way of "**welcoming**" me... I glanced over at her face. She didn't have the sort of mischievous face a person would have after doing something bad. Instead, she was biting her lips, as though she was forced to deceive me against her will.

I asked her, "Who told you to do this?"

She didn't answer, but she was shooting sideway glances at Gemma.

It was Gemma! She was angry that everyone ignored her so she made Matilda help her. She probably wanted revenge on me. How evil could she be?

I marched right up to Gemma's seat and shouted:

"You're such an evil person. You gave me ginger candy, fully knowing I hated it, just because you wanted everyone's attention? Come on! Could you have been more creative? Ever since we were classmates, I knew you were a cruel person!"

After I finished denouncing her in front of the class, I noticed everyone was staring at me. It was awkward so I explained to everyone what happened. They all sympathized with my position and pitied Matilda.

Later, at lunch, I asked Matilda if she wanted to be my friend so Gemma wouldn't bother her again. She said yes immediately. Then we went to find Ms. Hayes to tell her about the incident.

Ms. Hayes was taken aback. She claimed that Gemma always looked so "**cool and chill**" that she never would have guessed she would do such a thing! Ha, ***so cool and chill…*** I then told Ms. Hayes that I used to be classmates with Gemma when we were in kindergarten, and that she was a big bully.

She was speechless. Her face turned pale. She told

us to leave her office and tell Gemma to come in. We walked past her in the corridor and told her that the teacher wanted to see her. My heart was racing. Who knew what that maniac would do after hearing the news?

She said, "If I'm in trouble, ***you two are dead!***"

She walked away. The way she threatened us gave me the creeps.

Later that night, Matilda called me. She told me that her friend, Erica, happened to walk past Ms. Hayes's office and overheard what she said to Gemma.

"Erica told me that she heard Ms. Hayes scolding

Gemma, saying she shouldn't behave like that anymore. She said that Gemma should stop being a bully and try harder on her own grades."

I doubt that she would change. She WAS a bully when we were at kindergarten. All these thoughts scrambled in my head. ***Well, we'll see tomorrow!***

Chapter 3
Me for Revenge

After this affair, I was still angry. So, I started a kind-of-a revenge plan. First, I made friends with the entire school, even the principal.

The next day, I started to talk to every person in our class: Erica, Aleina, Adeline, Aline, Savana, Julian, Charlie, Adrian, Easton, Brater, and so on. I made friends with Grant and Joshua, hoping to use their good brains to help me craft my revenge plan. I also made some strong friends, like Savana and Rowan, in case Gemma wanted to beat me up.

With someone as daring as Tamriel on my side, I would never have to be afraid of Gemma. Nothing scared him, not even a lion. He could just shout at Gemma and ***voilà!*** She would be scared away!

I was worried that Matilda was feeling left out. I felt guilty, but I didn't mean to give her the cold shoulder. I talked to her.

"Um, hey, Matilda. I know I haven't been talking to you recently, but I really did not do that on purpose. I'm sorry. **REALLY** sorry," I said.

"Well, why didn't you talk to me when you know you could be talking to me?" She questioned.

"You know I had to make friends with a ridiculous amount of people to get some sweet revenge for the both of us. Maybe even the whole school." I answered.

"But I tried to help organize the whole thing, yet you just pushed me away and said 'Matilda, later. I'm busy now.' And you wouldn't even hear me out."

"I'm really sorry. I have a kind of weird behavior that makes me harsh towards others whenever I get busy or become too focused on something. I've tried to make myself better, but I just couldn't. And now, I'm seriously-really-extremely-very-incredibly sorry," I apologized.

"Fine. Why do you just have that kind of magic that makes everyone forgive you? Just, next time, make sure you let me know." She answered, smiling.

"Thanks," I responded genuinely.

She understood and forgave me. Now that the problem with Matilda was gone, I could keep on my revenge plan.

One of the customers of my mom's manicurist was our principal's sister! I could be friends with the principal easily, and maybe, I could even take over the principal in the future! Then I would be able to easily ***expel*** Gemma from the school! Ha! My imagination was running wild! Well, it was worth a try!

I formed a gang called ***G.R.G***, which stood for ***Gemma Revenge Gang***. I invited all the people in school, even the principal. Obviously, I hadn't invited Gemma!

G.R.G
G.R.G
G

We made many rules. The most important rule of all was: ***NEVER TELL GEMMA ABOUT THIS GANG.*** It was actually pretty hard to hide about this gang.

We had a secret code, Goose. I basically just chose this because both goose and Gemma start with ***G***. And Gemma was why we started this gang. So, that made sense!

Chapter 4
A Sentimental Sunday

I heard that Gemma came from a single family, with only a dad that didn't really seem to care about her. Mean, right? So, I decided to research this: Will children become a bully if they didn't get enough love from their parents? Turns out, they did! ***So I was thinking, maybe—just maybe—she became a bully because of her dad? Perhaps, but it was too soon to make a judgment.***

The next day, I went to Gemma's house. I knocked on the door, and a huge, gigantic man opened it.

That man must have been her dad. He gave off me a mafia boss vibe. His hair was shaped like a sharp hill, and he had a scruffy beard. He wore his sunglasses indoors, which I didn't know what for.

"What?" He groaned in a loud and low voice.

"I'm Gemma's classmate, Samantha, —May I talk to you? Mr. Hoffman?" I asked politely.

"It's Darris. Come in," he said.

When I went into Gemma's house, I was surprised to see how fancy and expensive the decorations all were! I had never thought Gemma's family would have collected so many valuable paintings! So many famous paintings, like ***Dora Misa, The Berry Sight, and Boy with a Rat***

Earring!

We sat down.

"What are you here to discuss? Is there something wrong with Gemma? She's always been such a good kid." asked Mr. Hoffman.

"So you think she's been behaving well the whole time?" I questioned, scoffing at the idea that she had fooled her dad well enough.

"Of course! And she even told me there's a new girl in class! Though she says that she's super dumb! Ha!" Mr. Hoffman cried.

"Do you know who Mr. and Mrs. Lawrence are?" I asked.

"Oh~~Yeah, yeah, yeah, yeah~! The Lawrence family, you know, Gemma used to always bully their little daughter. I wonder why. Oh, because she was such a ***goody-two-shoes!*** You know her? 'Cause, let me tell ya, she's disgusting!" Mr. Hoffman responded.

"**I AM that goody-good girl you badmouthed.**" I shouted angrily, "And that's what I wanted to tell you too! Ever since that first sentence about Gemma blurted out from your mouth, I knew you weren't paying a lot of attention to her! You don't even know a single thing about her. A good father always knows about his kids, but you don't. **YOU**'re the one who's disgusting. You think I'm disgusting because you don't even know how disgusting your own daughter is, you **cray-cray!** Gemma always picked on me in kindergarten, but now, she even picks on my friend, Matilda Welson!"

I was furious, but I was curious too. ***I had never***

seen or even heard of dads like this.

"Listen kid," he stared at me sternly. "I've been working so hard just to give my precious Gemma a perfect life. Her mother died when she was only two years old. She started to feel depressed ever since the funeral. I promised myself that **I would do whatever it took to give Gemma a good life!**" He shouted angrily.

Despite my raging anger at this man, I could still tell the words he spoke were genuine.

Just then, Gemma walked past us and stared at me. Oh right, I forgot today was a Sunday. She probably would be at home.

"Why are you guys shouting at each other? And Samantha, why on Earth are you in my house? Shouldn't you be at Matilda's and be playing some ***little girl*** things!" Gemma demanded, staring at us in anger.

"I'm sorry, Gemma. I didn't know you were here. I just wanted to talk to your dad privately..." I said in a quiet voice.

"Gemma, she was just saying you were a big bully and you were disgusting!" Mr. Hoffman exclaimed.

"Why do you **ALWAYS** have to interfere with my personal matters? Just be the ***goody-two-shoes*** you are and stop sticking your nose where it doesn't belong!" shouted Gemma, annoyed.

I was exasperated. "Okay, fine. You know what? When I was

in kindergarten, I held out hope that one day you could see me as a friend. Do you remember the nice things I did for you? But instead, you bullied me. You **laughed**, **bullied**, and **mocked** me!" I cried, my tears dripping.

Gemma and Mr. Hoffman were dumbfounded. They gave me some tissues to wipe my tears. They started to whisper.

"Oh, this is gonna be embarrassing", Gemma murmured, "Calm down Samantha! Don't be such a crybaby. Your tears are dripping on the carpet, and it's making it dirty. Just go home and I'll try to think. I guess…"

I could tell that her voice was friendlier.

Chapter 5
The One and Only Frenemy

When I got home, I told my parents what happened at Gemma's house.

"I think Gemma's not a bad person after all. I mean, her mother passed away when she was two, so that could be a reason why she had so much pent-up anger issues." said my dad.

"You're right, that may be why. Also, her dad never really had time to spend with Gemma." added my mom.

"I think I'll have a good talk tomorrow with

SL

you-know-who. A very non-emotional talk." I said, determined to resolve things with her once and for all.

"Aww, Samantha Lawrence, you make us proud!" exclaimed my parents in unison.

I was too excited to sleep. ***I rolled, I kicked, I rolled, I kicked.*** And I repeated it again and again. But when I was doing that, I was also thinking. ***Maybe Gemma didn't have to stay my enemy forever. Maybe, she could be my one and only frenemy. Like in the Ruby and Her Goblin series.***

The next day, I tried to become frenemies with Gemma.

"Uh, hey Gemma! I'm sorry about yesterday. I was just really curious about how someone like you became a mean girl…" I explained.

"***Nah***, it's okay." She answered, seemingly a bit awkward from our exchange yesterday.

"Well, we might have started on the wrong foot. Do you want to try being frenemies starting now?" I asked.

"***Frenemies***?" She questioned.

"Y'know, like friends who are also enemies. Like, something in between," I explained.

"Then I guess we can be '***frenemies.***' I guess." She replied.

"Oh, oh. Ok. Can't believe you said yes," I said under my breath.

Now, we were officially frenemies. But I saw something funny! The moment Gemma and I decided to be frenemies, I saw Matilda in the corner, with her face scrunched up like a rolled-up ball of trash. She frowned at me. ***Huh?***

I was at a loss why she was looking at me like that but I decided to pay it no attention.

While Gemma and I got closer day after day, Matilda and I grew further apart. Well, you absolutely couldn't blame me. If anyone was to blame, it'd be Matilda. She didn't seem to talk to me or even bother me now. She even got along with the most annoying girl in class, Amara! I knew she was just trying to annoy me. I was actually thinking about being friends with Gemma instead of Matilda!

But, ***Nah,*** that was probably not gonna happen.

Chapter 6
Principal Bad

As you know, I was frenemies with Gemma now, which means I needed to disband G.R.G.

Every student, every teacher, and every person in our school agreed. Well, everyone but the principal. The janitor, Mr. Phail, even tried to go to the principal's office and persuade him to change his mind. But the stubborn principal wouldn't bother.

"It cost a lot of money to make this gang. You asked me to make badges and jackets! You literally pleaded with me, on the first day of this gang, saying, 'Oh, Mr. Castillo, please join the gang! If you don't, many students definitely won't come to school.' End of story. So, no. Never. Even if you gave me my favorite ***Hawaiian pizza***, I won't change my mind."

With a flick of a switch, I suddenly had an idea. Since Hawaiian pizza was his bottom line, maybe if I baited him with ten boxes of Hawaiian pizza, he might actually change his mind!

When I got home, I explained the situation to my mom and asked if I could order ten boxes of pizza as it was the only hope I had to solve this dilemma.

"Of course, dear.

That's a pretty unreasonable principal you have. Go ahead and take your phone and call for pizza delivery," my mom responded.

The next day, I carried the pizza I ordered and marched right up to the principal's office.

"I demand you to agree to listen to my suggestions" I said.

"Or else what," he asked, looking a little bemused.

"Or else, you won't get this stack of pizza!" I demanded, holding it up high, as though dangling bait above fish.

"Never! I will never bow before you!" He was stubborn.

"Um… maybe some more pizza?" I asked.

He didn't answer. Instead, he turned around and

Pizza
=DISBAND?
??????

thought in different, deliberate poses for about 10 minutes.

"Then that's a deal, Samantha Lawrence!" The principal exclaimed.

But the trouble didn't stop there.

Chapter 7
The Board Makes a *D*ecision

I was very sure that you have never met this kind of principal. The kind of principal that was sly enough to make you want to call the police.

The next morning the principal gave us, people who were in the hallway, a little speech through the school speaker.

“Everybody listen up. Today is the day that I need to make a new school law. **Law #30l: Never kick your principal out of a gang.**

"Now, is this new law engraved in your brains yet? Hum? Samantha Lawrence?"

That sly principal! That moment was super-duper awkward. About too-many-that-I-can't-count pairs of eyes were staring at me.

When I got home, I told my mom to call the board of the school 'cause the principal was positively ***MAD!*** I made fun of the principal in front of my mom.

She agreed, she even said, "We need to send Mr. Castillo to court!"

Mr. Castillo was our principal's name. (That was why our school was called Casteral Elementary School. His family had been running this school for many generations.)

My mom helped me cancel today's class, so we could go find a lawyer. Yeah, no. This was completely false. ***Ding! Ding!*** The real reason I canceled school today was because the board of the school wanted to talk to me, as I was probably the one who was gonna save everyone from that evil principal!

"Hi! My name is Zadic Zuperman…So, your name is Samantha Lawrence, right? I'm from the board of Casteral Elementary School, as you know. And I've received a report from you detailing the misconduct of Mr. Castillo. Tell me about it," said Mr. Zuperman.

"Well, it's a long story. So, I had formed a gang to promote awareness about bullying, and I invited Mr. Castillo, too. Not long before, I disbanded the gang as it had served its purpose. Everyone agreed, but he didn't. I knew he loved Hawaiian pizza, so I decided to order 10 boxes of pizza to deal with him (because without it, he probably wouldn't have listened to a single thing I had to say). With the pizza as a bargaining chip, he said yes, but the next day, he insulted me in front of everyone on the school speakers. He even created a new school rule that was directly in response to what I did!" I cried.

"Oh no, principals can't make up their own regulations! I shall discuss this with the board. I'm very curious about what you said, Samantha. When we first interviewed him, he said he was gonna be a **fun** and **good** and **kind** principal, and we didn't know that he was going to go against everything he set out to do," Mr. Zuperman spoke with great disappointment.

The next afternoon, the board called us.

"I'm sorry, there are ten people on the board of Casteral Elementary School. But, only nine people agreed. So, because we need to follow the rules, if we don't have a unanimous vote, then the trustee needs to make the final verdict. So, do you agree or disagree?" Mr. Zuperman asked.

"Of course, I agree! Dude, is that even a question?" I said.

Yeeeeeeeeeees! We were finally free! ***Ring! Ring!*** Oh, the phone was ringing.

"We still have one more thing to tell you. There's another rule. If the principal of Casteral Elementary School gets fired, the person who takes over this principal job has to be someone who has experience with leadership positions. Well, we can't find anyone because our own special system is broken. So we tried finding one of Mr. Castillo's friends and was hoping someone would say yes to this powerful job, but no one said yes. Then, we thought of you, who was quite the important person in this whole *'Mr. Castillo gets fired'* thing. And here we are. So you're gonna be the new principal. You can be principal for life if you want to. But you must have an adult to make sure you're not doing something crazy. You can do whatever you want, but you can't add rules by yourself. Or you will get fired. You get to wear your own clothes and bring your own lunch. You still have to go to class, though. Oh, and you won't get paid. Only adults get paid. That's what all adults have been workin' for," said Mr. Zuperman.

"**O-o-okay. Thank you,**" I said, with a shaky and

shocked voice.

I stood there for a minute. When my mom and dad came over, I finally spoke to them.

"I-I am th-the new pr-pr-principal of school."

When I finished, I fainted.

When I woke up, I was lying on my bed, thinking hard. I was the new principal of school! How exciting was that! Mr. Zuperman said I couldn't make my own rules, but that was okay. I could still do so many things!

As usual, I set my alarm clock and went to sleep.

Chapter 8
There is a Main Messenger Behind?

Ring! Ring! The alarm went off. It was 7 am. This was a brand-new start for the school and me.

When I was getting ready for school, I chose my own clothes, 'cause I was the principal and I didn't need to care about uniforms! I ate my breakfast 'till 8 o'clock. Soon, I would be a principal.

When I walked into school, Gemma came up to me and asked, "Why are you wearing your own clothes? Mr.

Castillo would be mad!

"You don't need to worry about him anymore, 'cause I'm the principal now." I said, proudly.

"What? No way!" Gemma said, "You were still a student on Tuesday, and now, you're telling me you're a principal! That's insane!"

"Well, why don't you go to the principal's office and see for yourself!" I offered smugly.

When Gemma came back, she cried, "Everyone, listen to me! I have some really important announcements to make. Now that Mr. Castillo has been fired, we have a new principal! And the new principal is none other than Samantha Lawrence!"

The students in the hallway gasped. Everybody stopped what they were doing. Books were dropped to the floor because some students even used their hands to cover their mouths. There were murmurs like **"No way!"** and **"That's impossible!"**

From the corner of my eye, I saw Matilda scowling at me. Was she jealous? Or was she angry? Never mind, I didn't need to care about her anymore 'cause I was the principal! I marched right up to my office and sat in the chair. ***Ahh~*** It felt ***so good*** to be the principal!

I convened a meeting in the morning.

"Because the principal is a kid like all of you, that means you're gonna have more fun than before," I announced.

The students gave a round of applause, and it was very loud and enormous. I was off to a good start.

"1. Students can leave school whenever they want, but only after 2:45 p.m.

2. Students can wear their own clothes at school, but only on Mondays, Wednesdays, and Fridays.

3. Every student needs to pick two hobbies in class, 'cause the classes you'll take on Tuesday and Thursday will be cross-curricular.

4. Every Friday there will be a ***Show and Tell.*** Everyone needs to bring a thing to share.

5. Wednesday is movie day, so remember to bring some snacks.

Everyone clear?"

"Yeah! You're the greatest principal in history, Samantha!"

chorused the students.

Well, I was happy, they were happy, that was good! Wait a minute, was that Matilda The Miserable Face? Oh no, she was walking towards me! I couldn't move! I was terrified of what was to come, and I didn't know why.

"Matilda—***Woah!***" I hadn't even finished talking when she dragged me backstage.

"I know what you are doing, trying to impress everyone in school, so you can make everyone think that you're a good principal. You think they won't tell the board that you make the rules, but ***I*** will! Oh, I will tell the board, everyone that works for our school. I will not miss anyone. Then ***I*** can be the new principal. And I will make sure to torture every student in the school because ***I detest you.***"

I was ***flabbergasted.*** That was way too cruel. Why did she even hate me? I thought we were still acquaintances, even if we weren't the closest of friends anymore. I didn't care much about the words Matilda told me. She couldn't possibly do that, right? ***Nah,*** she wouldn't do that.

After this little conversation, I wanted to make my office comfier, that was what I was thinking about. So I ordered two bean bags, a beautiful rug, a really big and nice bookshelf, a cabinet for video games, and another cabinet for my stuffed animals. After four or five hours, I was finally done. My office turned from a plain office into a comfy, beautiful one.

The bean bags were for the students and me. For

students, when teachers told them to go to my office, they could sit on the bean bag while they listened to me talking. For me, I could sit on my bean bag or hanging chair and read, play video games, write stories, and sleep.

The next day, I saw some people from the board walking towards the main entrance of school. ***Maybe they were checking on how the school works 'cause there was a new principal,*** I thought. I welcomed them by giving them some fresh fruit to eat. Then I gave them a tour.

"These are our classrooms. As you can see, these classrooms are decorated by a unifying theme. For example, if it's the art classroom, there will be famous paintings hanging on the walls. There will be blank canvases hanging all around the classroom, waiting to be painted on by our creative and artistic students. Or, if it's a science class, the classroom wallpaper will be themed to resemble a laboratory." I explained, "On Tuesdays and Thursdays, students can go to extra-curricular classes. If they want to sing, they go to the little music rooms. If they want to draw, they go to the art rooms.

"On Monday, Wednesday, and Friday, the students wear their own clothes, so they can show off their sense of personal fashion.

"On Wednesday, it's movie night. Well, this whole

event isn't really at night, it's just more interesting this way. I made movie night because I believe students can't just study all day long. They need to relax sometimes. And on Friday there is a ***Show and Tell***."

They nodded, then a girl said, "Nice to meet you! I am Delilah. I just want you to know that we came here because a student called me yesterday, she said you were making school laws. I thought you knew better, but I guess you don't. So, we decided to fire you."

"***What!?*** I didn't make any ***rules***, I was just telling the students what they *can* do. These are two totally different things, you know! I understand and know the existing rules clearly," I shouted. "And was the girl who told you this whole thing called Matilda?" I asked.

The answer was a resounding **yes**.

So after all, it was Matilda. Always acting so innocent, but deep down, she was evil. You could never judge a book by its cover.

"I know, but we still have to fire you." Delilah said.

"No! I already told you, I haven't been establishing any hard-set rules. My orders don't have to be written and memorized by the future generations. I'm telling them what to do."

"You do have a point. But what if there won't be another principal? What if you get to be principal for life? Students these generations would just ***'follow your orders'*** for decades! Then what did we fire Mr. Castillo for, right?" Delilah said.

"Fine. But can you guys do me one favor?" I asked reluctantly.

"What is it?" Questioned Mr. Zuperman.

"Can I be principal for just one more month? Please. I want all of us to relax while I'm still the principal. Also, who knows if the next principal is gonna be as crazy as Mr. Castillo!" I begged.

The board huddled into a small circle— I supposed — to discuss my appeal.

"Yes, you can. But only for one **month**. That's all." said Delilah.

I thanked them and they left.

I told everyone the announcement immediately.

"I have something important to say. I will be principal only until next month. So I hope you guys can cherish the time you can to relax, doing ***Show and Tells***, wearing your own clothes, and watching the movies you enjoy. Thank you."

I turned off the microphone and I fainted. Not that my heart stopped literally, but it was just that I was really sad that I could only be principal for ***one month***. And my legs went numb.

But before that, I still had one thing to do: To find out why Matilda would do this to me. Why she would be so cruel to me?

Chapter 9
Another Meaningful Gang

To figure out why Matilda would be so mean and cruel to me, I was going to start another new gang. I knew this gang would be disbanded perfectly because I was not inviting people that didn't listen to me.

The announcement about the gang spread all over the school. Everyone came to my office to join. Of course, not including Matilda, though. There were some rules in order to join, including: you can't be dumb, and you can't be time-wasters…

Knowing this, I prepared some slightly more specific questions for the candidates. Luckily, most students passed. I was surprised that Gemma got in, but I didn't show the whole shocked expression on my face, because I thought that might end up offending her and we'd become enemies instead of frenemies again.

Anyways, I scheduled the meetings needed to discuss the matter. The list looked something like this:

First time:
December 20th, 2022

Second time:
December 22nd, 2022

MEETINGS:

First time:

December 20th, 2022

Second time:

December 22nd, 2022

Third time:

December 26th, 2022

Fourth time:

December 28th, 2022

Five time:

December 30th, 2022

Sixth time:

January 2nd, 2023

Seventh time:

January 4th, 2023

Eighth time:

January 6th, 2023

Third time:

December 26th, 2022

Fourth time:

December 28th, 2022

Fifth time:

December 30th, 2022

Sixth time:

January 2nd, 2023

Seventh time:

January 4th, 2023

Eighth time:

January 6th, 2023

That was all the time I could squeeze in.

First Meeting...

"Listen to me now. This is our first meeting, and the only thing I want you guys to know is that there are no rules for this meeting. And that's all. So let's get started. I wanna ask, who knows Matilda's personality? Like, very well?" I asked.

Somebody raised their hand. Oh! It was Jessica...

"She always acts nice when you're friends with her, but when you're better than her, she turns evil and she'll be cruel to you. She will try to destroy you and get rid of you if she can, no matter what." She added quickly as an afterthought, "Oh, but not that cruel. I might be exaggerating it a bit. I'm known to be more than a little dramatic, as you know."

I didn't know if I should be scared by the first part or relieved by the last part.

"How did you know?" I asked.

"Well, first, I was friends with her, so I know she definitely can be nice on the outside. But then I realized she was actually more cruel than I thought she was because when you and Matilda were backstage, I heard all the words she said to you," responded Jessica.

"Ok, thanks for the info." I said.

It was weird that everyone literally heard what

Matilda did. Well, looking on the bright side, at least they didn't know what she said to me, right?

"Now, let's talk about the gang name. Any suggestions? It needs to be about revenge, detective, investigation, and intelligence," I stated.

"Sackers," a boy said.

"***Revengergators,***" Grant said.

Immediately, I agreed on this name because I want revenge and we were probably going to become investigators to find out the truth of the "Matilda Mystery."

Ring! Ding! Oh, the dismissal bell has rung.

"Everybody needs to go home now. See you tomorrow."

Second Meeting...

"Any ideas why Matilda is acting weird recently?" I asked.

"Maybe because you've been mean to her maybe once or twice?" Aleina suggested.

"No, not once. Although I've given her the cold shoulder before. But that was just because I needed to manage some important business," I said.

"Ooh! Ooh! I know, I know. Maybe it's because you don't spend enough time with her," said Joshua.

"Well, that may be the reason. But I don't think that's why 'cause she was my only friend when I transferred here. But, when I was spending more time with Gemma, I was kind of not talking to her…" I said.

Actually, I was starting to think that I really needed to spend some more time with Matilda lately. You know, so I could make it up for her.

"Well, I think she's been hypnotized. I watch *Maptain Cucumber* all the time, and he turned into the character because Meorge and Carold ***'did the thing'*** to Mr. Bump, who was actually Maptain Cucumber. So my point is Matilda may be hypnotized by someone," said Gemma, "I mean, I watched the show when I was young, not really watching it now though," she clarified.

I kinda thought she added the last sentence because she didn't want everyone to think that she still watches *Maptain Cucumber*. Yes, but that unnecessary clarification made it even more obvious that she still watched that cartoon. Also, she did say "all the time."

"I don't think that's the problem. And if hypnosis were real, that means the person that hypnotized Matilda needs to be very good at doing it." I replied, "We don't know if there are people that can do hypnosis. I actually think that could be plausible, but it'd only explain a fraction of her behavior. But we'll just keep that in mind for now."

Third meeting...

"Now, let's continue what we did last meeting." I said.

"I think the main reason is that she's a psycho," said

Destiny. She was from another class.

"What? What? No, no, no. That's impossible. I think **YOU** are the one who's a psycho…" I whispered.

I mean, she WAS kinda coo coo!

"You said **WHAT?!**" She shouted.

"Nothing," I replied.

"I know what you said. And you know what you said. I'll take revenge when you least expect it."

Great. Another enemy. Hmm… Maybe Matilda and Destiny would be great friends. ***The Enemies of Samantha…*** Ha! That would be funny.

"Other ideas?" I asked.

"I know," said Tamriel. "I think she's jealous of you."

"That's why we're here," I sighed. "The whole point

of these meetings is to find out ***why*** she is jealous of me hanging out with Gemma or becoming principal. ***Duh~***" I exclaimed.

Wow, I really like to say "duh." ***Duh~*** I need to stop, it sounds rude. ***Duh~*** Ok, stop it! Stop it!

Everyone laughed. Except for Tamriel who was probably still out of the loop.

"I still think the reason is that Matilda's hypnotized," said Gemma.

"I told you, that's impossible. But we can still keep this as a working theory," I said.

I wanted to know why Gemma kept mentioning this. It couldn't be true, could it? Because Maptain Cucumber was just a cartoon.

Chapter 10
Meetings, Meetings—Woah!

Another week full of meetings. I was actually bored right now, you know. The same people saying the same things, over and over. But it was December 29th, so the meetings were almost over.

Fourth meeting...

"Ok, I'm starting to think Matilda is really hypnotized by someone, since nobody's got a better and plausible idea." I said.

"What? That's not fair, I have an idea, I just haven't said it yet," Samuel, my neighbor, exclaimed. He paused for a minute.

"Well, if you have something, say it!" I groaned impatiently.

"I'm gonna say it, uh—it's just I can't remember what I was gonna say," he said.

"Don't waste our time, you clown!" I shouted.

Everyone laughed. Naturally, Samuel didn't laugh. He scowled at me. ***UGHHHHHHH!*** Another enemy. And I bet he was gonna soon join "***The Enemies of Samantha***".

"Other ideas?" I asked tiredly.

Being a principal was quite tiring. You would

understand it if you were a principal.

"I got one," said a random first-grade girl.

Her eyes wandered for a minute. And she still didn't say anything! For goodness' sake, why did all first graders need to wait so long to talk? Like seriously, **WHY?**

"**T-A-L-K! Talk!**" I said.

"Okay. I will talk." She answered, "Wait, I'm chewing my gum."

Ughhhh! Even first graders were chewing gum now?

"Just spit it out on a tissue!" I hollered.

"Why should I have to?" She demanded.

"As a matter of fact, this is a meeting. So why are you eating gum in the first place? This is becoming such a total drama!" I exclaimed.

"Fine." She finally spit out her gum on a tissue, "My idea is that she really thinks you're rubbish. And *so do **I**,*" She retorted snarkily.

"Hey, don't say that. That's sad..." I said.

"Well, sorry!" She scoffed.

"I'm sorry too. You'll have to do detention with Mr. James later today for being rude. Remember, I'm your principal," I stated.

"Whatever. I'll just skip detention." She murmured.

"Okay, now, **REAL** ideas! Real!" I cried.

"Come on, why don't you just believe me that Matilda was hypnotized by someone!" Gemma shouted.

"**Nooooo. NO.**" I said, "I'm never going to bow before Maptain Cucumber."

"Now, no more ideas?" I asked.

"No." chorused the students.

"Well, you guys better think of some ideas that you can present tomorrow..." I said.

That really was a total disaster.

Fifth Meeting...

"Okay students, this is the fifth meeting. And still, no one has any great ideas for me," I said.

I looked at the students in the hall. They were the himbos of the school. Well, some of them weren't, but wait a sec, wasn't that Matilda? So she had been listening to us the whole time? OMG! She must have been fuming.

"Matilda, I'm so sorry. I-I can explain." I said. "Can you come up here and accept my apology?" She walked up to the stage and just stood there…drooling?

"Matilda? Hello? Excuse me? **ALOHA AAAA!** Can you even hear me?" I asked.

I thought she was sleepwalking. I meant, how could someone be drooling unless they were asleep?

"**You annoying-poor-second-rate-bad principal!** How ***dare*** you talk about me that way!" She roared.

"Matilda, I think your eyes aren't working normally right now, do you need to go to the doctor?

You see, there're circles in your eyes, as though you're hypnotized." I said.

"Hypnotized, hypnotized... ***You're hypnotized!*** " I exclaimed.

"Told ya. I'm definitely a genius." Gemma said.

"Ok, don't brag. I can't really believe she really is hypnotized... It seems we need a plan to catch the person that hypnotized her and try to wake her up."

"I have a plan. Ok, listen. First, we need to find where Matilda lives. Then, we sneak into her room and try to catch the mysterious guy," Gemma said.

"And?" I asked.

"There's no ***'and'***," she scoffed.

"Ok, that's that but who knows where she lives?" I asked.

"I know, but I'm not gonna tell you unless you say that Maptain Cucumber is the best hero ever in history," Gemma declared.

Why did she need to be so obsessed with Maptain Cucumber? I was starting to think that **SHE** was hypnotized.

"Why are you obsessed with Maptain Cucumber? I still don't get it!" I cried.

"Uh, um, oh! So are you gonna say that Maptain Cucumber is the best hero ever in history?"

Great, now she was changing the subject.

"Fine, I'll do it because I want to know who hypnotized Matilda, not because Maptain Cucumber is really the best hero." I said.

"But he is!" Gemma whined. "Fine. The address

is on Mana Street. I remember it's a brown and white house."

"Now, shall we wake her up?" I asked. The students suggested snapping or clapping my hands to try waking Matilda up. The first try didn't go as easily as I expected.

"Try and snap your fingers, Samantha!" Shouted Grant.

Snap! Snap! That was supposed to wake her up.

"Matilda?" I asked carefully.

"***You annoying-poor-second-rate-bad principal!*** How ***dare*** you talk about me that way!" She roared a second time. Ok, she repeated the same things again.

The second try was much better.

"Oh, it didn't work. Try clapping your hands!" Shouted Joshua.

Clap! Clap!

"Matilda?" I asked even more carefully this time. I didn't want Matilda to judge me with ugly language.

"Um, Samantha? Why am I standing on the stage? And why is everybody looking at me?" She said.

"Matilda! Your eyes are normal again! I'll tell you the whole story. It's very long. Make sure you're prepared." I exclaimed.

Chapter 11
Gotch'*y*a!

"Ok, now. Let me ask you, do you remember who Mr. Castillo is?" I asked.

"Yeah, he's the principal who insulted you in front of everyone!" She cried, "Right?"

Great, now I knew she wasn't hypnotized until I became principal.

"And, do you know that I'm the new principal?" I asked.

"Wait, what? Really? No way! Does everyone know

this?" Matilda cried.

Now, that was just me making sure that I calculated the right time.

"They know. And do you know that you were hypnotized the whole time when I was principal?" I asked.

"No. Definitely not." She said, "But I definitely remember that Gemma picked on us."

"And do you remember where you live?" I asked.

"'Course! I live on Sunny Avenue, in a brown house." She answered.

So, Gemma lied to me just because she wanted me to say that ***Maptain Underpants*** was the best hero ever? Oh, come on!

After I finished lunch, I stomped over to her seat.

"Why did you give me the wrong info about Matilda? If I hadn't asked Matilda again, we would have gone to the wrong house!" I shouted.

"Huh, really?" She said, "Oh~ That's my cousin's dad's friend's daughter's boyfriend's mom's house!"

"Your cousin's dad's friend's what?" I shouted.

"My cousin's dad's friend's daughter's boyfriend's mom's house," she answered.

"Okay, so your cousin's dad's friend's daughter's boyfriend's mom's house?" I asked.

"You're good at memorizing things!" She exclaimed.

"Thanks, I— Wait, that's not the point." I said, "It's wrong to lie to people just to get what you want."

"Yeah, whatever. Sorry," Gemma apologized, while

making a weird face.

"Okay, should we reconvene a meeting to make a plan about how we should find this mysterious person?" I asked.

"What mysterious person?" She asked.

"The person that hypnotized Matilda!" I cried, "What's wrong with you?"

"Sorry," she said.

In the afternoon, I convened a meeting.

"Okay, who has a plan for finding the person who hypnotized Matilda?" I asked.

"Me! Me!" Malcon cried, "Okay. So, we know where she lives, right? Later, when it's nighttime, we hide in her bedroom and catch the guy!"

"Great idea! Now, who wants to go with me?" I asked.

OMG, so many people raised their hands! Who was I going to pick? We, well, I wanted, two boys and two girls, there was me in the team already, so there were two boys and one girl left to choose.

Well, Malcon was Matilda's brother, so he knew the house. And Barrett, he was a tough guy. Now, for the girls, I prefer Erica. She was on the martial arts team in school!

"Quiet now. Thank you. I've decided to let Malcon, Barrett, and Erica go with me," I declared.

"Yes!" Malcon and Erica cried.

"But I don't want to go. I didn't even raise my hand," Barrett protested.

"Fine, who wants to replace him?" I asked.

"***Meeeeeeeeeeeeeee!***" Grant shouted.

"Sure. Remember it's tonight, okay?" I said.

"Right!" Malcon, Erica, and Grant exclaimed.

We met at 9:00 P.M. tonight. At Matilda's house.

"Okay, now— Where's Malcon?" I asked.

"I think he's inside." Grant said.

"Well, let's go in and find him. He might be wearing his PJs." I said.

He **WAS** actually wearing his PJs in the living room waiting for us to come!

"Oh, hey guys! I kept watching TV to keep me from sleeping," he said.

"Oh wow! It's kind of a good idea! So now that everyone's here, shouldn't we start step 2?" Grant asked.

THE PLAN:

STEP 1:
→ Go to her house

STEP 2:
→ Hide

STEP 3:
→ wait for "IT" to show up

STEP 4:
→ Erica& Gayden fights "IT"

STEP 5:
→ wake up their parents

STEP 6:
→ call cops

"Yeah, let's hide!" I exclaimed.

We hid in different places in Matilda's bedroom. Malcon hid in his bedroom, which was closer to the door because he thought that the guy might try to escape. I hid in her closet, Erica hid under her bed, and Grant hid in her bathroom.

We waited 'till the guy came. Oh, ***it was 11:00 P.M. already!*** Why hadn't he or she come? We waited for 10 minutes. Then— There was a noise! I bet it was him (or her) trying to break into Matilda's bedroom.

I made a sign to Grant and Erica to tell them that "the guy" has come. They nodded at me and got ready.

Knock, knock! Suddenly, the door opened and the guy just stood there, looking at Matilda.

Grant and Erica ran towards the guy when he wasn't

looking. I ran out silently to warn Malcon while Erica and Grant fought the guy.

When we rushed back, Matilda was woken up, and the mysterious guy had already been taken down by the two of them.

"Great job, you two!" I exclaimed.

They clapped hands to celebrate.

"Now let's see who's under that mask." I said.

Malcon pulled his face mask off and to everyone's shock and horror, it was Mr. Castillo!

"***Mr. Castillo?***" we cried.

"Oh, hey guys. Miss me?" he asked shamelessly.

"Absolutely not!" we shouted in unison.

"Hmph! That's harsh!" he exclaimed.

"So you were the mysterious guy we've been trying

to catch all along?" Erica asked.

"Aren't you smart!" Mr. Castillo said.

"Why did you do this to Matilda?" I asked.

"No, the question should be **why I was fired!**" he yelled at me.

"You'll hear all about it when we're at the police station," I answered.

"Malcon, find Mom and Dad!" Matilda exclaimed.

I followed Malcon to his parents' bedroom. And I saw them arguing!

"What are you talking about? I've never heard of someone who can hypnotize someone!" Malcon's dad cried incredulously.

"Follow me and you'll know!" Malcon shouted in exasperation.

When their parents were in Matilda's bedroom, they were shocked. "What the heck is going on…" They muttered under their breaths.

"Mr. Castillo? What are you doing in my house? And have you seen someone acting suspiciously?" Malcon's mom asked.

"***He*** is the guy who hypnotized me, Mom!" Matilda cried.

"Oh my gosh, call the cops!" Her mom screamed.

Ten minutes later, the police came. An officer called Officer McKlane arrested Mr. Castillo. She asked us questions like "How did this happen" and "Do we have any eye witnesses?"

"Well, I don't know, I guess he just knew how to hypnotize people," I said.

"As for me, I also noticed that Matilda was strange at first, but I thought she was acting that way on purpose," Erica chimed in.

"**Ughhhh,** there's no **useful** evidence!" Officer Mcklane exclaimed in exasperation.

Just then, a tall, black man walked into the room. He said his name was Officer Kapow. ***Kapow!*** Ha, it sounded like such a fun name!

"Hullo, Officer McKlane!" He said, waving his hand.

"Oh, hey! Didn't see you coming in!" she said, waving her hand back.

Officer Kapow

probably liked Officer Mcklane because his cheeks and ears went red when she waved back.

"Can you help me interrogate these little children? I can't find any useful evidence!" she cried.

"Sure, I have nothing else to do! What's the case?" He exclaimed.

"Number 20164, Castillo." Officer Mcklane said.

"**Ahhhhhhh!** He's the worst!" He yelled.

"What's wrong with him? I thought he was just an ordinary principal who's always up to something mischievous," Matilda asked.

"You really want to know?" She questioned.

"Of course, we're always prepared. Nothing can faze us now," we said, firmly.

After one hour of crazy explanation, we finally

realized that Mr. Castillo wasn't just an ordinary principal who was "up to something mischievous." He was a criminal, **a real criminal!** Well, a petty thief to be fair. But still, he drove officers crazy in the past! ***So that was why Officer Kapow was so afraid of him.***

Still evil! Wait, I forgot to tell you something. We learned that his actual name was Parondacky Quint. That was insane, right? Like, what kind of parents would name their children Parondacky? That was kind of wacky if you ask me.

When it was 2:00 A.M., it was decided that Mr. Quint was to go to trial. I hoped he got jail time for at least 5 years. We separated and went back home.

Chapter 12
Normal Now, Normal Life

We were back to normal, now that I was not principal, Matilda was not hypnotized, and Mr. Quint was in jail, and there was no weird business going on. Gemma was also finally no longer obsessed with Maptain Cucumber anymore…

"Hey, have you found the burglar yet?" Gemma asked me.

"Yeah, turns out, it was Mr. Castillo, and his real name was Parondacky Quint!" I answered.

"**HAAAAAA!** You must be joking, ha… Wait, you can't be serious?" Gemma replied.

"When am I **NOT** serious? Anyhow, are you ready to be friends with Matilda?" I said.

"Do I really have to? Like, we're solar opposites!" Gemma cried.

"Yes, just think that it's for me. I like both of you, but you guys don't get along!" I pleaded.

"Fine," Gemma groaned. "But you have to say that Maptain Cucumber is the best hero ever in history."

Well, I guess I was wrong. She was definitely still obsessed with Maptain Cucumber.

"Why lord? **Why??** Why does Gemma need to be so obsessed about Maptain Cucumber?" I yelled. Everyone in the cafeteria stared at me. It was **sooo** awkward.

"Because you want me to be friends with Matilda, and I am not the kind of person that agrees on everything without a deal!" Gemma exclaimed with a wide grin on her face.

"Do I really have to?" It was now my turn to groan.

"Yep. And you need to say it out loud so that everyone in the cafeteria can hear you." Gemma said.

"Ughhhhhhhh!" I groaned again.

"Say it, say it, say it!" She shouted.

I stood up on the table and shouted,

"MAPTAIN CUCUMBER IS THE BEST HERO EVER IN HISTORY!"

"Get down there right now!" The cafeteria lady yelled at me.

"Sorry," I apologized, my face flushed red with

embarrassment.

"You were yelled at by Ms. Sherry! Haha ha haha!" Gemma started laughing at me.

"Don't laugh!" I said.

"Okay, we got a deal." Gemma replied.

"So, go ask Matilda!" I exclaimed, embarrassed.

As Gemma walked away from the cafeteria, I sighed deeply. What a semester!

The next day, rumors had spread out that Gemma and Matilda were friends. Well, this time the rumor was actually true!

Okay, this semester was about to end and things are slowly returning to normal. Although I was not fully prepared for the next semester, I still have a whole winter break to prepare right? If things were already this out of hand this semester, how could next semester be any crazier?

SOMETHING
ABOUT MY CLASSMATES

G

Hey, it's me! Samantha! First, I want to say: Don't you think this semester is full of mysteries and fun? I do! Well, look, sometimes I want to blame Mr. Quint for making us get in trouble, but I can't. He actually made this fun semester without even knowing.

Anyways, I want to say thanks for reading the whole story. And now, I am gonna share the secret files of Grant, Erica, Matilda, Gemma, Mr. Castillo (of course!), and me. ***Mwahahaha!*** (Actually, it was not that secret…)

Grant:

- ✓ Birth: March 29th, 2013
- ✓ Nationality: Canadian
- ✓ Gender: Male
- ✓ Personality: Smart, aggressive, funny
- ✓ Height: 4 feet 7 inches

Erica:

- ✓ Birth: October 27th, 2012
- ✓ Nationality: Canadian
- ✓ Gender: Female
- ✓ Personality: Brave, kind, trustworthy, pretty, bright
- ✓ Height:4 feet 6 inches

Matilda:

- ✓ Birth: April 10th, 2013
- ✓ Nationality: English
- ✓ Gender: Female
- ✓ Personality: Respectful, truthful, pretty, a bit bossy to everyone, confident
- ✓ Height: 4 feet 7 inches

Gemma:

- ✓ Birth: October 30th, 2012
- ✓ Nationality: American
- ✓ Gender: Female
- ✓ Personality: Protective, always nice to her friends except enemies, likes black, not very smart but it's good enough
- ✓ Height: 4 feet 10 inches

Mr. Castillo:

- ✓ Birth: January 17th, 1955
- ✓ Nationality: American
- ✓ Gender: Male
- ✓ Personality: mean, short tempered, dramatic, dull
- ✓ Height: 6 feet

Me (Samantha):

- ✓ Birth: October 21st, 2012
- ✓ Nationality: Half American, half Asian
- ✓ Gender: Female
- ✓ Personality: emotional, bright, popular, creative, dramatic
- ✓ Height: 4 feet 6 inches

Something About You: